The ghost who eats the toast

By

Neil Kirby

&

Rachael Kirby

Don't be afraid, this is fun!

The Ghost Who Eats the Toast.

One morning I did go downstairs.
To find no bread for breakfast there.

My mom and dad deny the theft.
As I look at simply breadcrumbs left.

I'm sure there was the night before.
Now, just the wrapper on the floor.

Lots of times and not just one.
The bread has vanished, simply gone.

Something weird is happening here.
Something strange, peculiar, queer.

Tonight, I plan a trap to find,
Who's driving me out of my mind?

The night-time comes and darkness falls.
I yawn I'm tired but suspicion calls.

I make a trap, to find the oaf.
The one who steals my crusty loaf.

I wait and wait, but then I find,
I'm just too tired, losing my mind.

Next thing I know, I'm coming round,
With sunny daylight all around

I've missed the thief who steals my bread.
I Lost my loaf, I slept instead.

My bread has gone, not one slice left.
I feel so angry, sad, bereft.

I won't give up, I'll try again.
Ill set the trap to ease this pain.

A fresh new loaf, the bread thief bait,
With creamy butter on a plate.

I clear the pantry and place in a chair.,
A place to hide, won't be seen there.

I sit and wait, I'm eager now,
I'll will catch this bread culprit somehow.

In gloomy darkness, I sit and wait,
The clock strikes twelve, it's very late.

And suddenly I see a glow,
Quietly gliding, moving slow.

Is this the culprit, the bread thief?
As I rub my eyes in disbelief..

"I have you now" I shout and mock.
The culprit halts as though in shock.

On goes the light, the room now bright,
I see the thief with good, clear sight.

I can't believe what I can see.
A ghostly sheet in front of me.

I watch and stare frozen with dread.
As the ghost picks up my loaf of bread.

It then makes toast with butter spread.
Scoffs every piece of toasted bread.

The ghostly sheet is clear to see.
But something odd appears to me.

As I look down below the sheet.
I notice slippers upon its feet.

With one good pull, I now can see.
Its not a ghost in front of me.

A harmless girl, with long brown hair.
My little sister standing there.

With all the noise and carry on.
Appears my dad and then my mom.

They start to laugh at what they see,
My bread thief stood in front of me.

My sister's laughter loudest most,
As we sit around enjoying toast.

I told you there was nothing

to be afraid of!

The end...

Printed in Great Britain
by Amazon